W9-AZY-590

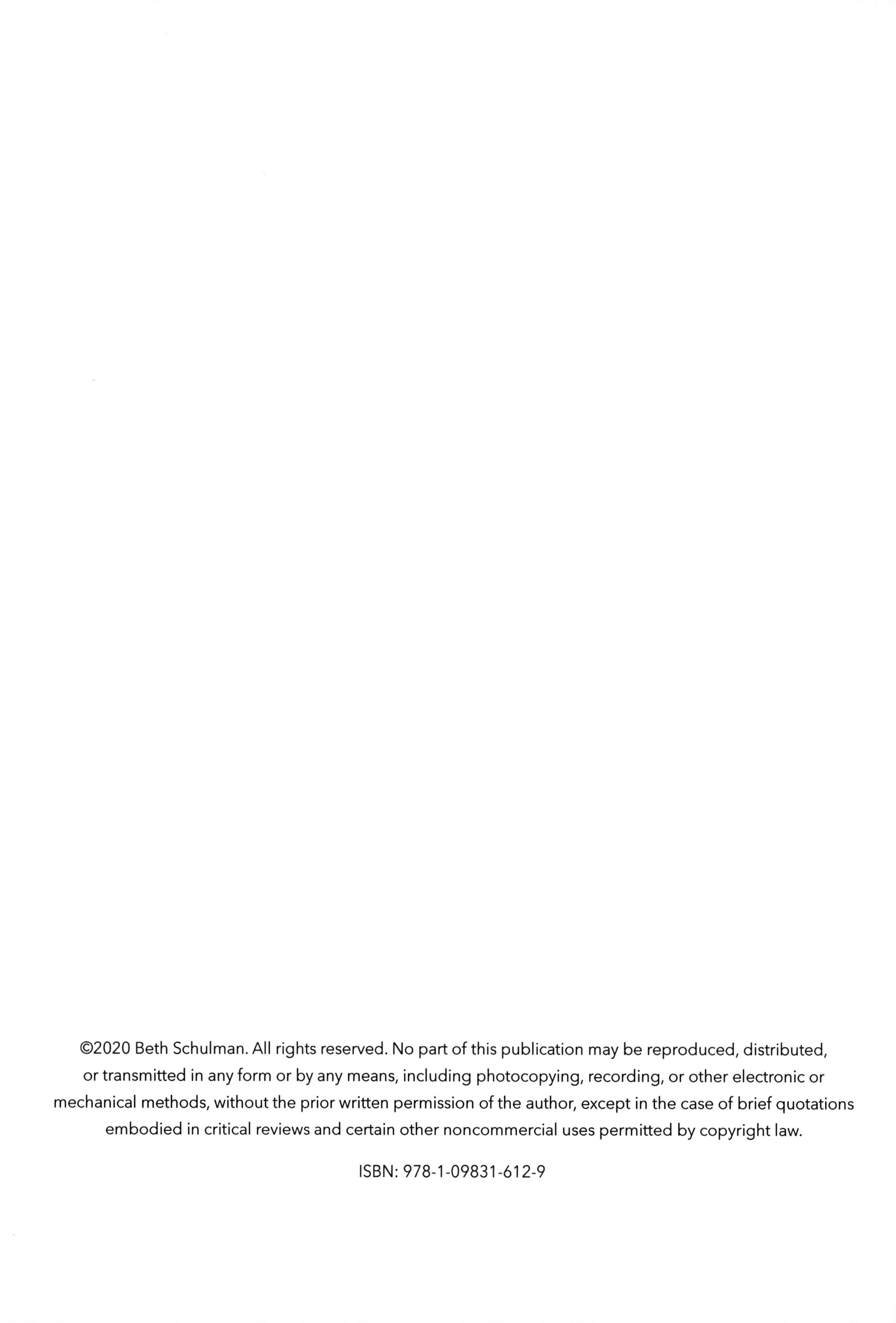

ISBN: 978-1-09831-612-9

The Cardboard Castle

Written by
Beth Schulman

Illustrated by
Sherri Bausch

The morning bell rang. I felt like I was half asleep probably on account of the heat. It was hot and humid. The big thermometer, hanging from the rusty nail on the concrete wall of our classroom read ninety-five degrees. This was no surprise, since it was the beginning of June. By the end of the school year, Washington Elementary felt less like a school and more like an oven. As soon as I sat down, my thighs stuck to the chair. My mind wandered out of the classroom and into summer. I could almost feel the cool water of the city pool splashing on my face.

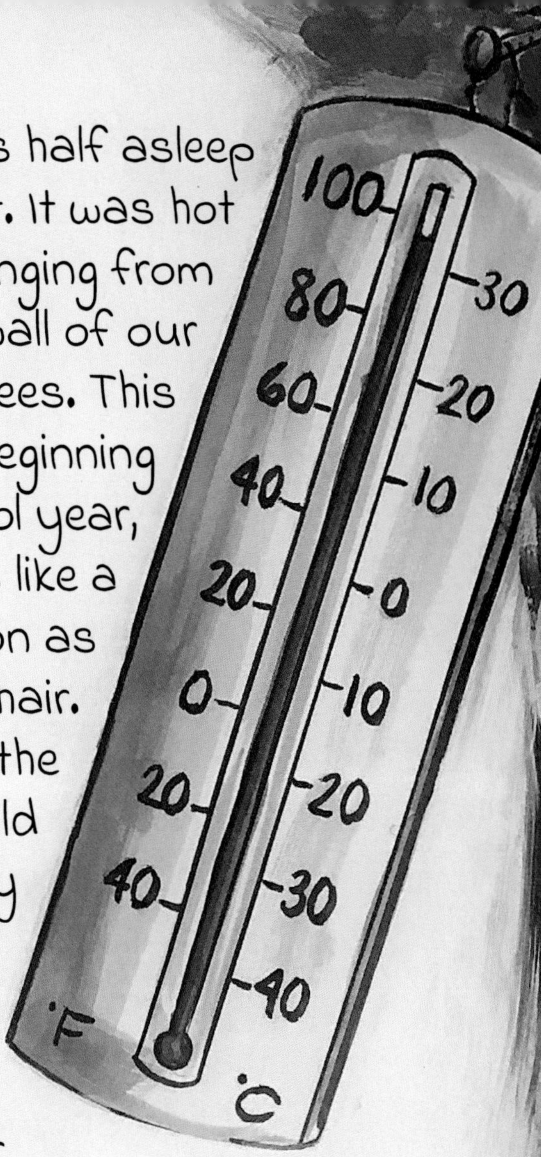

Mr. Govern, our fifth grade teacher, tried to open the windows. Two wouldn't budge and the other three opened just a crack. Not even a hint of a breeze could squeeze through. Mr. Govern made his way over to the light switches and turned them all off. "There we go," he said, "now the room will stay cooler." We all knew that turning off the lights wouldn't change the temperature in the room, but we played along. Mr. Govern was one of the few teachers who smiled when we came in each day and never yelled. He was always saying stuff like, "There's no i in team! Let's work together!" and "Si se puede- yes you can!" He was our favorite teacher.

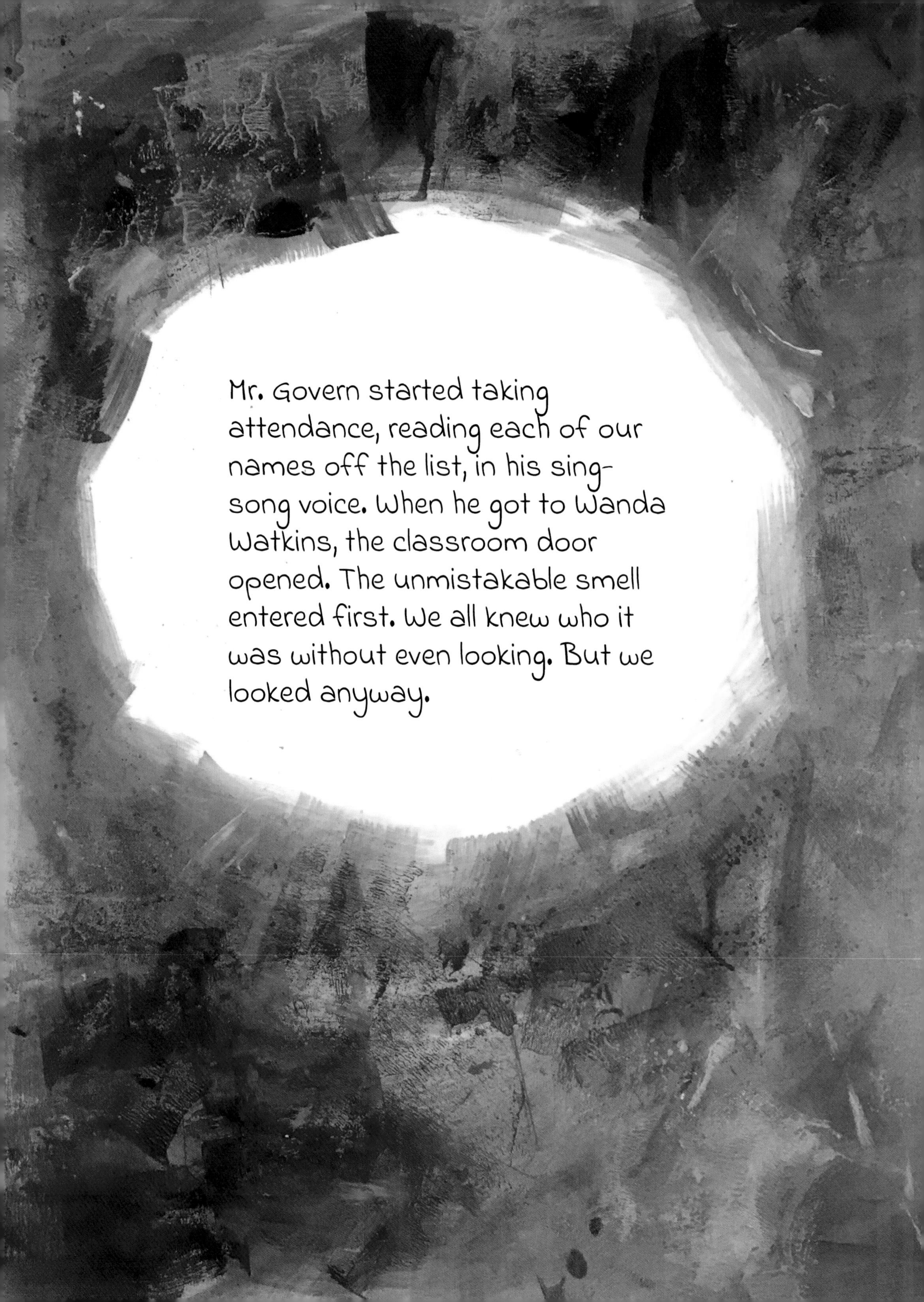

Mr. Govern started taking attendance, reading each of our names off the list, in his sing-song voice. When he got to Wanda Watkins, the classroom door opened. The unmistakable smell entered first. We all knew who it was without even looking. But we looked anyway.

Twenty-eight pairs of eyes stared at Stinky Stella who stood like a statue in the doorway.

Stella's long dark hair had a permanent knot in the back that looked like a nest for a small bird. Her nails were lined in dirt; and despite the sizzling temperatures, she wore the same jeans every day. She smelled like old gym socks. We were in second grade when Kiara started calling her Stinky Stella.

Stella had been in our class since kindergarten. There was only one class of each grade at Washington Elementary, so we'd all been together for the past six years. Well, not exactly all of us. There'd always be a couple of kids who'd start in the beginning of the year and then leave sometime before we got to June. Like this year, Louis moved into our class in September and by Halloween he was gone.

But Stella had been around since kindergarten. Even back then everyone knew she was different. Most of us lived in the two blocks around Washington Elementary in the attached brick row homes surrounding the school. Stella lived three blocks past the corner store, the place we were told not to go.

"P-U!!!"
Dante' squealed, holding his nose between two fingers.

"That's enough, Dante," Mr. Govern said in a serious tone.

Then Mr. Govern did something we never saw him do.

He just stood there.

Perfectly quiet.

We waited. And waited.

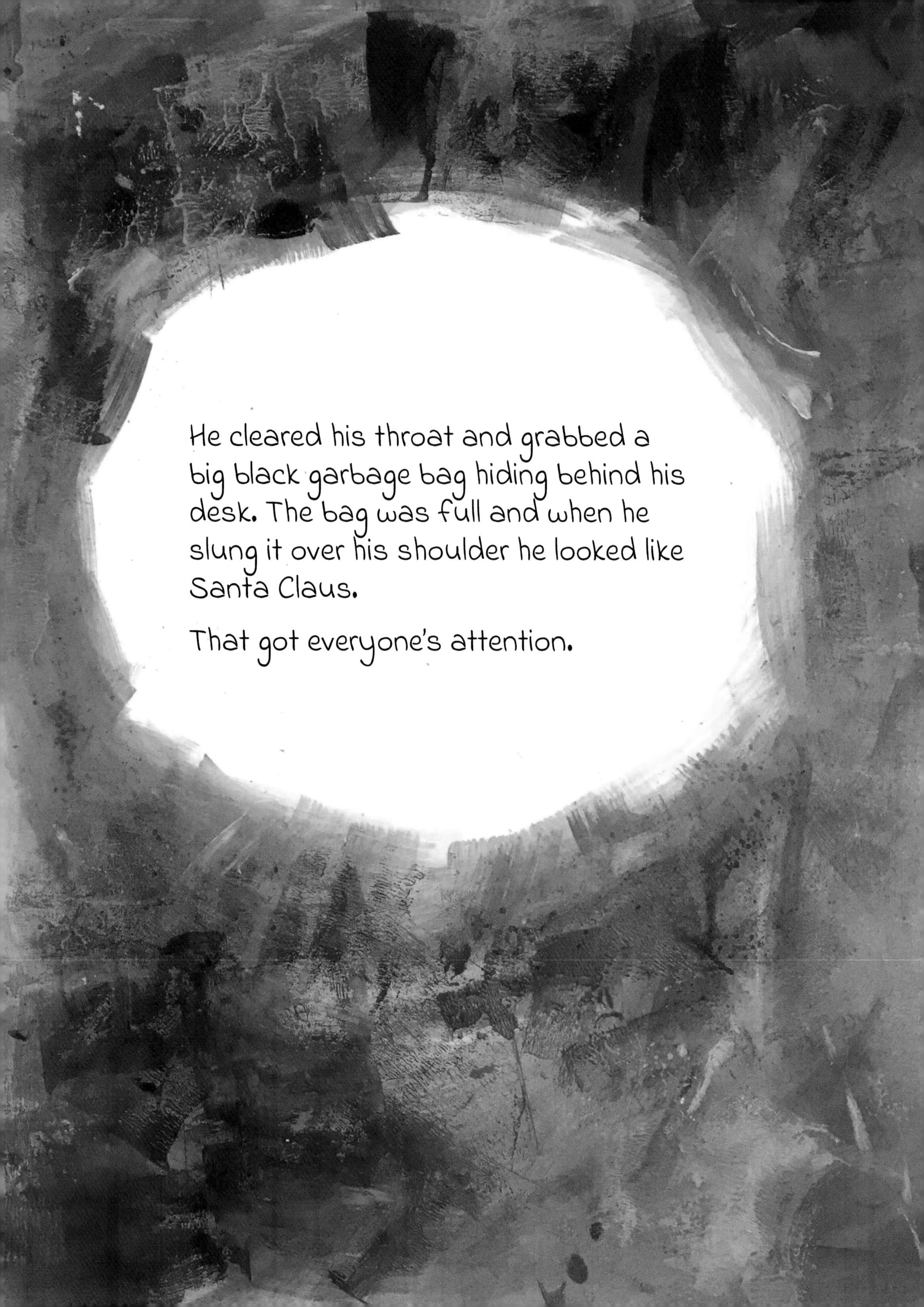

He cleared his throat and grabbed a big black garbage bag hiding behind his desk. The bag was full and when he slung it over his shoulder he looked like Santa Claus.

That got everyone's attention.

"Yo, Mr. Govern!" Javier shouted from the seat behind me,
"What's in the bag?"
Javier's question unleashed an eruption of chatter.
"You got presents in there for us?"
"New balls for recess?"
"Got any jump ropes?"

Mr. Govern stood there calmly holding the bag. He was a small guy with dark brown hair. Some of the boys in our class were already taller than him. He raised his arm over his head, giving the quiet signal--two fingers up. A large spot of sweat stained the armpit of his white, buttoned up shirt.

The class got quiet and Mr. Govern spoke.

He stretched out each word, speaking in a slow, measured tone.

It was like staring at the ketchup bottle turned upside down, wondering when the sweet red stream would appear.

We shifted in our seats, feeling the itchy discomfort that comes from waiting.

"Today, my friends, we become architects."

He reached into the bag pulling out one box at a time.

A shoe box. A juice box. A cereal box.

Finally he turned the entire bag upside down, leaving a mountain of boxes in the front of the room.

"We are going to construct our own city. Build a house, an apartment building, a restaurant. Use your imagination! Be creative! All supplies on our art shelf are up for grabs!"

Since it was June, the art shelf was looking pretty sad. There was a can filled with scissors and another filled with mostly dried out markers. A small pile of faded construction paper sat next to a few half filled bottles of Elmer's glue.

"What are you waiting for?"
Mr. Govern's voice got louder.

"Pick a partner and start creating!"

Within seconds the energy in the room shifted.

Boys and girls buzzed around, calling out names of the friends they wanted to work with. My best friend, Maria, found me right away and pulled me toward the art shelf. We picked through the sparse supplies and ended up with a pair of scissors, two markers, one purple and one blue and a piece of red construction paper so faded it actually looked pink.

By the time we got to the front of the room where Mr. Govern had set up the boxes, most of them were gone. I found one shoe box and Maria grabbed an empty juice box. All the kids huddled together in pairs around the classroom, stacking and cutting and glueing.

Everyone except Stella. Stella sat at her desk and laid her head down.

Juice
C
PURPLE
SIZE 9

Mr. Govern walked over to her.
I could hear him talk to her in a real quiet voice.
"You can join one of the groups," he suggested.
"No one's gonna want me in their group," she answered without lifting her head from the desk.

"I can ask Maria and..."
Mr. Govern started, but Stella interrupted.
"If it's okay with you, I just wanna rest."
Mr. Govern paused for a moment and then said,
"Sure Stella, no problem."
I let out a sigh of relief. I kinda felt bad for Stinky
Stella, but I didn't want to be stuck
working with her.

Hotel
MILK

When the bell rang for lunch, Maria and I had just finished our project.

We'd drawn little rectangle shaped bricks all over the faded red paper and glued it to one side of the shoebox. We stuck the juice box on the front and drew on a blue door knob. We gave each other high fives.

After lunch, we each got a turn to go up to the front of the room to share our creations with the class.

There were tall buildings and short buildings and square houses with rectangle shaped roofs. Eva and Kim had even added a front porch to their house!

While we oohed and ahhed over each creation, Stella sat at her desk, slumped over, drawing with a stubby pencil on a piece of notebook paper. She never once looked up from her paper to see what we'd all made.

At dismissal time, Maria and I stayed behind to clean up.

We noticed Stella standing in front of Mr. Govern's desk.

"I saw a big box sitting at the curb on my way to school today. If it's still there, do you think I could take it and do the project at home?" Stella asked.

"That's a great idea. Here, come with me, Stella."

Mr. Govern grabbed the black trash bag, now empty, and led Stella to the back of the room. He used one of the keys he wore on the lanyard around his neck to open the closet.

Maria and I watched as the opened door revealed shelves packed full of art supplies. We couldn't believe our eyes! Stacks of brightly colored construction paper, rolls of colored cellophane, sleeves of tissue paper, and jars of paint in every color, crammed the crowded shelves. It was like a secret rainbow had been hiding behind that door!

"These supplies are for next year, but I want you to take whatever you need,"

Mr. Govern whispered.

He handed her the trash bag and without saying a word, Stella started to fill it up.

"Can't wait to see what you create," Mr. Govern said, winking at Stella and giving her a soft pat on her back.

Glitter

PUBLI SCHOOL

The next morning Stella got
to school early.

I was surprised to see her already sitting at her desk when I entered the room.

Small groups of kids were standing around, talking and pointing towards the front of the room.

That's when I saw it.

A giant cardboard castle.

It looked like it had been plucked right from an enchanted forest, taken directly from the pages of a fairytale!

"Stella created this castle and I'd like her to tell us about it, " Mr. Govern announced.

The class collectively held their breath.

Dante' started waving his hand back and forth, but before Mr. Govern could call on him he shouted,

"No way! That's awesome!"

Stella walked real slow to the front of the room. Her head hung low and she didn't look at any of us. When she got to the front of the room, her voice was a whisper.

"A little louder," Mr. Govern prompted gently.

Stella's voice rose just a little.

None of us said a word.

The room was still.

We listened.

Stella shyly explained how she'd painted various shades of grey in circular strokes to make the box look like it was covered in stone. She pointed to the colored windows that looked like stained glass, telling how she'd made them from cellophane.

The more Stella told us about her castle, the rounded towers with intricately painted turrets, the drawbridge that really folded down, the more animated she became. Her voice grew stronger, her eyes sparkled and a big smile spread across her face.

We continued to listen attentively, our eyes wide and our mouths slightly opened.

When she finished speaking the entire class stood up and started to clap.

The clapping got louder and louder.

Then we all raised our arms high above our heads and cheered in unison,

From that day forward, no one ever called her *Stinky Stella* again.

Instead, everybody knew she was "Stella, The Artist."

I called her Stella, *my friend*.

Stella
the
Artist!!!

A Note from the Author

The Cardboard Castle is based on a true story a dear friend and fellow teacher shared with me about his first year teaching in Philadelphia. As soon as I heard it, I knew it was meant for a wider audience. I wanted to retell his story in a way that would encourage important conversations in the homes and classrooms of our children.

If you are a parent or teacher, here are a few discussion questions to get the conversation started.

Which character are you most like?

Describe a time when you were teased or treated unkindly. What happened?

What did you do?

What would you do if you saw a student in your class being teased like Stella?

If you were a student in Stella's class, what could you do to make Stella feel included?

What do you think life at home might have been like for Stella?

Do you think Mr. Govern was a good teacher? Why or why not?

There's an expression, "Don't judge a book by it's cover?" What does this mean, and how does it relate to this story?

About the Author

Beth Schulman has devoted her life's work to creating supportive, literacy rich learning environments for her young students. She teaches from the heart and believes every classroom should be a place where students feel respected and celebrated. She lives and teaches in the Philadelphia area. Schulman has taught in the public school system for over 25 years. She has worked with professional teachers through The Penn Literacy Network at The University of Pennsylvania as a literacy coach and instructor since 1997. In addition, Schulman has been an adjunct professor of Child Development and Language Arts Instruction in the Master's of Education Department at Chestnut Hill College in Philadelphia.

Schulman is the author of the children's book *Rosie, The Practically Perfect Puppy* (2017) inspired by her dog and two sons and *The Gold Mailbox, a memoir* (2016). Her own personal story is reflected in *The Cardboard Castle*. In her memoir, Schulman writes, *"We're all shaped by our experiences. I wouldn't be the person I am today without having lived through the trauma of my childhood. It wasn't easy and there have been many hurdles along the way. But my past has brought me to the place I am today, a place of compassion, love and deep gratitude."*

Schulman hopes *The Cardboard Castle* inspires that same compassion, love and deep gratitude in her young readers.

About the Illustrator

A Pennsylvania native, **Sherri Bausch** now lives, teaches and creates in Los Angeles, California, and has supported and inspired thousands of students, teaching in both public, private and collegiate settings. Currently, she teaches classical drawing and painting, and educates individuals about approaching and integrating the practice of art through energy, mindfulness and meditation techniques.

With a Bachelor's in Integrative Arts, and a Master's in Elementary Education, throughout her 25 year teaching career her focus on the arts as a vehicle for learning has supported and encouraged students, in both the academic and art classrooms in which she serves.

This is her first book illustration project, which she has approached "...as a labor of love and a dedication to the many children who feel they have something incredible to express to the world. *This story is so relatable for me, especially as a creative who really struggled to enjoy school in many ways. My best memories of the classroom are when we engaged in art projects–that's when I could really be myself and did well. My hope is that readers will engage with the book on many different levels and find the courage and inspiration to pursue whatever it is that brings them joy.*

Art
Glue
NEW